Wintertime

and The Cricket's Serenade

DANIEL HAMMAN

NEWMAN SPRINGS PUBLISHING
320 Broad Street
Red Bank, NJ 07701

First originally published by Newman Springs Publishing 2023

ISBN 978-1-68498-051-2 (Hardcover)
ISBN 978-1-68498-052-9 (Digital)

Printed in the United States of America

To my grandchildren

t has been years now since I moved into my grandparent's old house. I now have several grandchildren of my own, and every summer, they all come to visit me. And like me when I was a child, they listen to the fascinating stories that I tell them, the same ones that my grandfather once told to me.

Every day when they are here to visit, they play in the meadow and together we explore the same woods that I once explored all those years ago. They really enjoy the animals and walking down the path that leads to Herndon Pond.

In the evenings after dinner, we sit on the porch and watch the fireflies dance across the meadow.

But summer has long since ended and autumn has also come and gone. My grandchildren have each returned to their own homes. I am once again all alone in this old homestead. Winter has settled in. The snow has already covered the ground. The animals are now tucked away for the winter in their dens and nests. The beautiful music from Herndon Pond is no longer to be heard.

Now during the evenings, I sit on the porch and listen to the snow as it falls. It is amazing how the beautiful snowflakes can make a soft, calming sound as they fall to the ground while the moonlight shines across the snow-covered meadow.

At times, I will close my eyes while I am listening to the snow as it is falling, and I think back to the times when my grandfather would recite the poem *The Cricket's Serenade* to me. It is remembering those special times that has inspired me to write my own new version of the poem. It is entitled "Wintertime and The Cricket's Serenade."

The seasons have now changed
And winter has begun

My grandkids have all gone home
After a summer full of fun

I told them all of my grandpa's stories
And we explored the woods where I once played

Then every night, we would listen to
The Cricket's Serenade

HOOT
CROAK
HOOT
CROAK

The woods rest now in silence
The ground is a soft and silent white

The animals have all taken shelter
From the cold and bitter night

Herndon Pond is now frozen
No music is being played

The cold of winter has postponed
The Cricket's Serenade

But if you listen to the silence
You will hear a special sound

Of the snow as it is falling
So softly upon the ground

And the moonlight on the meadow
It dances where I once played

It's a nice replacement to
The Cricket's Serenade

HOOT
HOOT
CROAK
CROAK
CROAK

I look forward to the coming summer
And the music once again from Herndon Pond

With the crickets, frogs, and owls
All sharing a special bond

My childhood is now just memories
Of my grandma's lemonade

And my grandpa telling me the stories of
The Cricket's Serenade

I look forward to next summer when my grandchildren will once again come to visit. Their laughter and curiosity seem to always take me back to my childhood. Until then, I will enjoy the calmness of the winter and dream of the beautiful music rising from Herndon Pond. The music called *The Cricket's Serenade*.

The End